My Princess Collection

Pocahontas

Always in My Hea[rt]

Book Eleven

Written by M. L. Dunham

For information address Disney Press, 114 Fifth Avenue,
New York, New York 10011-5690.
Printed in China
First Edition
9 10 8
ISBN 0-7868-4604-6

For more Disney Press fun,
visit www.disneybooks.com

Chapter One

My name is Pocahontas. My father is Chief Powhatan, a fine and noble man, and also a wonderful father. Because he loves me, he worries about me. I am what he calls an independent spirit. I love to take risks—like diving off high cliffs into the water, and riding my canoe down rapids.

We live in a peaceful place in the woods near the ocean. The land gives us all we need to survive, and we love the peace and harmony that nature provides for us. Grandmother Willow is one of my best friends. She is a wise tree spirit who gives me advice and comforts me in times of need.

One day, I told her of a dream I had been having. It was a dream about a spinning arrow.

"Well, it seems to me," she said, "this arrow is to point you down your path."

But what was my path? What did the future hold for me?

It seemed the answer was not far away. You see, not too long ago, our way of life was threatened. Yet, along with that threat came something wonderful—someone, I should say, who changed my life forever. His name was John Smith. He arrived from the sea in a great ship with billowing sails that looked like clouds.

Chapter Two

Captain Smith arrived on our shores with a group of men who looked and acted differently than we do. We were frightened by them. They dug up our rich dark soil and destroyed our trees for no good reason.

They said they were searching for something called gold. At first, I thought they meant they wanted our gold-colored corn. I offered some to John Smith, but he said his fellow travelers were greedy and wanted a different kind of gold.

John Smith was different from the others.
I was drawn to him from the first moment I
met him. I could sense that he was a kind
man, although I knew that I should be careful.

But John Smith followed me. And when we talked at last, we found that we could understand each other . . . a bit.

"Please!" he said to me as I prepared to paddle away in my canoe. "I'm not going to hurt you." Then he helped me out of the canoe. Our hands touched, and I knew he was telling the truth.

Chapter Three

But John Smith was not perfect. At first, he wanted to change our ways by building us things called houses and streets. He wanted to make us "civilized." He didn't realize we loved our life the way it was. I was insulted and angered that he thought his people were better than mine. Yet I saw something in him that led me to believe that maybe—just maybe—he could learn to understand my people and our ways.

One day, I decided to show him all the beauties and wonders of the land around us. I pointed out how all the animals were my friends—and how the trees and plants provided both food and great beauty for my people.

By the end of our day together, John Smith
seemed to see the beauty in the simplicity of
our lives. He seemed to love our world . . .
and to be falling in love with me, as I was
with him.

Then, something terrible happened.

Chapter Four

Kocoum, one of my father's finest warriors, found me in the woods with John Smith. Enraged, Kocoum attacked my new friend.

When it was all over, Kocoum lay dead. It was not John Smith's fault, but that of one of his friends. Still, John and I knew that my people would blame him. And we were right. John was captured and was taken back to my father as a prisoner.

We knew that this was just the beginning. As tragic as one death was, this would start a war that would not end until many more had died.

Chapter Five

Soon after, John Smith was sentenced to death by my people. The settlers were ready for war in order to save John. My father wanted revenge for the death of his bravest, noblest warrior.

The two groups marched toward each other, ready to fight. I knew I had to do something—but what?

I raced to the wise tree spirit, Grandmother Willow, for advice.

"Remember your dream!" she told me.

I remembered the spinning arrow, and then I thought of John Smith.

"It was pointing to him," I said at last.

"It's not too late," Grandmother Willow advised. "Let the spirits of the earth guide you."

Chapter Six

I did as Grandmother Willow suggested. I ran to where my father was going to execute John. As my father raised his weapon, I threw myself over John. "If you kill him, you will have to kill me, too!" I cried.

My father laid down his spear.

Slowly, all the settlers put down their weapons—all except for one.

Suddenly, a shot was fired. To protect my father, John Smith pushed him out of the bullet's path, putting himself directly in the line of fire.

Unfortunately, John was gravely wounded and had to return to his home across the sea. I met him on the shore, just as he was getting ready to leave. My people joined me, bearing gifts for the settlers. We had found a place of peace between our two peoples at last.

As we said our good-byes, I knew John Smith was the man I loved. And I knew he loved me. I also knew that somehow, somewhere, we would meet again. As his ship set sail, I ran to the tip of a rock at the top of a mountain. I wanted to watch him for as long as I could . . . until his ship dipped below the horizon. And I vowed that no matter what it took, I would see him again, and that he would stay in my heart forever.